Written by Jo Windsor

Rigby

Look at these big animals.
These big animals are yaks.
Yaks live up in the mountains
where it is very, very cold.

mountains

Yaks have very thick coats.
Their coats help them keep warm.
A yak's coat can be very long.
It can go down to the ground.

When a baby yak is born,
it can hide in its mother's coat.
Her coat will help keep
the baby warm.

The people that live
in the mountains can use
the yaks for lots of things.

Sometimes people come to climb
in the mountains.
The yaks are used to carry things
up the mountain.

yak

People can drink the yak's milk.
They can make the milk
into butter and cheese.

People can eat
the yak's meat, too.

cheese

yak meat

People can use
the yak's hide to make things.
They use the hide to make
hats and bags.

bags

People can use yak's wool
to make things, too.
They use the wool to make
tents, boots, and other things.

wool

Sometimes people
use the yak's droppings!
They put the droppings on the fire.

Index

Guide Notes

Title: Yaks
Stage: Early (4) – Green

Genre: Nonfiction (Expository)
Approach: Guided Reading
Processes: Thinking Critically, Exploring Language, Processing Information
Written and Visual Focus: Photographs (static images), Labels, Index

THINKING CRITICALLY

(sample questions)

- Tell the children this book is about animals called yaks.
- Look at the title and read it to the children.
- Ask the children what they know about yaks.
- Focus the children's attention on the Index. Ask: "What are you going to find out about in this book?"
- If you want to find out about how people can use yaks' wool, on which pages would you look?
- If you want to find out about yaks' hide, on which pages would you look?
- Why do you think a yak would be better than a donkey for helping people in the mountains?

EXPLORING LANGUAGE

Terminology

Title, cover, photographs, author, photographers

Vocabulary

Interest words: ground, hide, droppings
High-frequency words: these, live, lots, that
Compound words: sometimes, into

Print Conventions

Capital letter for sentence beginnings, periods, commas, exclamation mark